Hermie
a common caterpillar

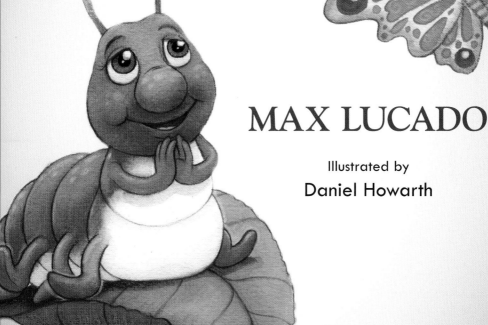

MAX LUCADO

Illustrated by
Daniel Howarth

Tommy NELSON®

A Division of Thomas Nelson Publishers

NASHVILLE   DALLAS   MEXICO CITY   RIO DE JANEIRO

Text © 2002, 2011 by Max Lucado.
Illustrations © 2011 by Max Lucado.

Karen Hill, Executive Editor for Max Lucado.

Illustrated by Daniel Howarth.

Published in Nashville, Tennessee, by Tommy Nelson. Tommy Nelson is a registered trademark of Thomas Nelson, Inc.

Tommy Nelson, Inc., titles may be purchased in bulk for educational, business, fund-raising, or sales promotional use. For information, please e-mail SpecialMarkets@ThomasNelson.com.

ISBN 978-1-4003-1747-9

The Library of Congress has cataloged the earlier edition as follows:

Lucado, Max.
  Hermie: a common caterpillar / Max Lucado.
      p. cm.
  "A just like Jesus story."
   Summary: Best friends Hermie and Wormie are sad each time they see that other creatures are special when they, themselves, are so ordinary, but they trust that they are *special* in God's eyes and that He is not finished with them yet.
   ISBN 1-4003-0117-3
   [1. Caterpillars—Fiction. 2. Self-esteem—Fiction. 3. Christian life—Fiction. 4. Friendship—Fiction. 5. Metamorphosis—Fiction.] I. Title

PZ7.L9684 He 2002
[Fic]—dc21   2002026439

Printed in the United States of America

12 13 14 15 LBM 6 5 4 3 2

Dear Parents,

Learning to read is a special time for children and parents alike. With every word your children read on their own, the magic of a story comes alive, and these stories open the door to a lifetime of reading.

From beloved author Max Lucado comes *Hermie a Common Caterpillar*. Now created in a Level 2 Reader format, a perfect starting point for readers-in-training, this book offers simple word choices and short sentence lengths.

With 5.5 million units sold, the *Hermie* series is a trusted brand parents can rely on for Christian messages told through humor and fun. As kids discover the joy of reading independently, they'll be learning how to love God on their own too.

Max Lucado has always had a passion for showing children how much God loves them. These new Level 2 Reader books are the perfect way to share that message with your beginning readers!

Happy reading!

Your Friends at Tommy Nelson

"Wow!" said Hermie the caterpillar as he looked at the tree above him.

A beautiful butterfly was resting on a large green leaf. His brightly colored wings were covered with dazzling white spots.

Hermie gasped and whispered to himself, "He's about to fly." And with a lift of his wings, the butterfly was in the air, circling softly in the summer sky.

"Oh, how I would love to fly like that," Hermie wished.

He watched until the butterfly was a speck in the sky. Then Hermie sighed and turned away.

Now, as a rule, caterpillars are not very exciting. But Hermie was even more ordinary than most.

Some caterpillars have spots. Not Hermie. Some caterpillars have stripes. Not Hermie. He had nothing but smooth green skin, some freckles, and a bunch of feet. Hermie was a common caterpillar.

He ate common leaves . . . squirmed through common grass . . . did common stuff. Hermie was a common caterpillar.

Hermie did one thing, however, that was *not* common. He talked to God. He talked to God about all sorts of things. And God talked to Hermie. Of course, he didn't really hear God speak out loud. God spoke in Hermie's heart.

Late at night when the other caterpillars were asleep, Hermie would crawl out of his bed and stare up at the sky. Then he would talk to God.

"God, why did You make me so common? Other caterpillars have stripes. Some have spots. I even saw one with spots and stripes. But me? I don't have anything. I'm just . . . Hermie."

"And I'm just Wormie," said a nearby voice. Hermie turned and saw a caterpillar that looked very much like him. No spots. No stripes. Another common caterpillar with freckles—his friend Wormie.

Once Hermie had told the other caterpillars that he talked to God—and they had laughed. But not Wormie. He understood. That's how they had become friends. Wormie talked to God too.

When Hermie and Wormie felt common, God would say, "Don't worry. I love you both just the way you are, but I'm not finished with you yet."

And so they would feel better . . . for a while. But then something else would happen, and they would feel common again. Like the day they met an ant named Antonio. Antonio was smaller than either of them, but on his shoulder was a big pinecone. They were amazed at the strength of the ant.

"My!" Wormie said. "How do you carry such a big load?"

"It's how God made me. He made me strong," Antonio answered. And off marched the tiny ant with the big load.

That night Hermie and Wormie asked God, "Why can't we be strong like the ant? We could never do what he could. Why did You make us so common?"

God's answer was the same as always: "Don't worry, Hermie and Wormie. I'm not finished with you yet."

And they felt better, at least until they saw a snail.

One afternoon, the sky opened up, and the rain soaked the ground. The two friends hurried as fast as they could to find a dry place. Suddenly, they heard a low, scratchy voice.

"Looks like you are in a hurry."

Hermie and Wormie stopped. They looked all around but saw no one.

"Did you hear something?" Hermie asked.

"I did," Wormie replied.

That's when Hermie saw a snail peeking out of his shell.

"Greetings," said the snail. "Looks like you are trying to get out of the rain."

"We sure are," Hermie answered.
"We're getting soaked."

"You need a house like I have," said the snail.

"That's your house?" Wormie asked.

"It sure is. Watch." And with that . . .

. . . the snail pulled his head into his shell.

"See it's nice and dry in here. I take my house with me everywhere I go," his voice echoed.

The two friends were sad. They wondered why God had not given them a cozy house like the snail's.

Later that night, Hermie and Wormie asked God why He gave the snail such a wonderful house but gave them nothing at all. "Why do we have to be so common?" they wanted to know.

Again, God's answer was kind and patient. "Don't worry. I love you both. And I'm not finished with you yet."

So they felt better. And for a long time, just thinking about how much God loved them made Hermie and Wormie feel special, and not so common, until . . .

. . . one day they saw a ladybug named Lucy.
Oh, what beautiful black spots she had! Neither
of the caterpillars had ever seen such spots. They
were perfect black, shiny circles.

"You have such pretty spots!" Hermie exclaimed.

"So black and shiny!" Wormie agreed.

"Oh, thank you," Lucy answered softly. Then the ladybug blushed, because she was very shy.

"I mean it," Wormie said. "We have never seen anyone with such beautiful spots."

"You are very kind," she replied. "But I had nothing to do with it. This is the way God made me."

Hermie and Wormie wanted to be grateful for the gift God had given the ladybug, but it was hard. Both of them felt so . . . common.

That night, underneath the bright stars, Hermie prayed. "God, we know You are good and wise. We know You love us just the way we are. But we don't understand why You made us like this. We're so very . . ."

"Common?" God said.

"Yes, common," both caterpillars answered.

"Remember," God told them, "I love you just the way you are. But I'm not finished with you yet."

Hermie sighed. He wanted to feel better. He tried to feel better. Usually, he did feel better. But that night, he still felt sad. He also felt tired. More tired than usual.

"Wormie," he told his friend, "I'm so, so sleepy.
I feel like I need to sleep a long time."

"Then let's make you a soft, comfy bed."

Once Hermie found the right leaf, he hung
down and closed his eyes.

"There," Wormie said to his friend. "Have
a good, long rest. I'll be waiting for
you when you wake up."

Hermie thanked his friend. Then he prayed to God and said, "You know, God, it's okay that I'm just a common caterpillar. You love me, and *that* makes me special."

Then Hermie drifted off to sleep.

As he slept, he dreamed that he was different.

He had strength like the ant.

He had a house like the snail.

He had spots like the ladybug.

He dreamed he was no
longer a common caterpillar but
something special instead.

After what seemed like a long time, he woke up. Everything around him was dark.

Hermie was covered from his head to his toes. What had happened to his comfy bed? He wiggled and squirmed to get out, and when he did . . .

. . . he and his bed began to fall.

Suddenly his bed cracked open, and
Hermie felt a tickle on his back.

Something wonderful happened. . . .
Wings fluttered open! Wings he didn't even
know he had.

They were wonderful, wide, colorful wings
with beautiful spots. And they were *his*.

Hermie stretched out his
wings, and then . . . he was
flying! Up and up, higher and
higher.

That's when Hermie realized what
God had done. Now he understood.
God had made Hermie special—
inside and out.

He wasn't like the ant . . . or the snail . . . or the ladybug. He was special! One of a kind! No one else was exactly like him. He was Hermie—a beautiful butterfly with a beautiful heart.

He soared high through the air, to the right and to the left. Then he thought of his friend Wormie. From the air, Hermie looked down at his broken bed. Nearby were the ant, the snail, and the ladybug. They were all talking to Wormie.

"Wormie!" Hermie called.

Wormie heard his friend's voice. "Hermie, where are you?" he called.

"I'm up here!"

Wormie looked up and saw a beautiful butterfly. "Hermie, is that really you?"

"Yes, it's really me."

"Wow!" said the ant. "You look so different."
"Goodness!" gasped the snail. "You are so big."
"Oh my!" admired the ladybug. "You are the most beautiful butterfly I have ever seen."

"God was not finished with me after all!"
Hermie said.
Then he flew down and
stopped right next to Wormie.

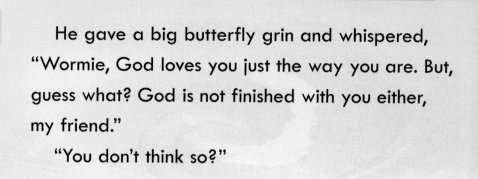

He gave a big butterfly grin and whispered, "Wormie, God loves you just the way you are. But, guess what? God is not finished with you either, my friend."

"You don't think so?"

"I know He's not."

"You know, you may be right. I'm starting to feel pretty sleepy too," Wormie said. Then he yawned a big yawn. And Hermie smiled a big smile.